PAUL ST

Neighbourhood
Witch

Illustrated by Annabel Large

VIKING

For Anna

VIKING

Published by the Penguin Group
Penguin Books Ltd, 27 Wrights Lane, London w8 5tz, England
Penguin Books USA Inc., 375 Hudson Street, New York, New York 10014, USA
Penguin Books Australia Ltd, Ringwood, Victoria, Australia
Penguin Books Canada Ltd, 10 Alcorn Avenue, Toronto, Ontario, Canada m4v 3b2
Penguin Books (NZ) Ltd, 182–190 Wairau Road, Auckland 10, New Zealand

Penguin Books Ltd, Registered Offices: Harmondsworth, Middlesex, England

First published 1994
1 3 5 7 9 10 8 6 4 2
First edition

Text copyright © Paul Stewart, 1994
Illustrations copyright © Annabel Large, 1994

The moral right of the author has been asserted

Typeset by Datix International Limited, Bungay, Suffolk
Set in 16/24 pt Monophoto Palatino

Printed in England by Clays Ltd, St Ives plc

A CIP catalogue record for this book is available from the British Library

ISBN 0–670–85116–7

CHAPTER ONE

Off With a Bang

We were having tea when it happened. Richard, Harriet and I (that's Thomas, in case you're interested) were busy dipping Marmite soldiers into our boiled eggs, Mum was sipping a cup of coffee, while Herbert – who spends more time asleep than awake these

5

days – was under the table, snoring. Nobody spoke. Nobody looked up. The atmosphere in the kitchen was so tense, you could almost see it.

The reason? Dad had just phoned from Tokyo to say that there had been a hitch in his business negotiations: he would be delayed a further week. Bang went our promised camping holiday. Bang went Mum's decision to confront Dad about Gran'ma.

BANG!!!

The deafening explosion from upstairs echoed throughout the house. It sounded as if the roof had come in. The effect in the kitchen was almost as dramatic. I dropped my spoon, Harriet bit into her tongue and began bawling, Richard fell off his chair and Mum knocked over her coffee. Herbert, who, being half-deaf, might have slept through

the actual explosion, certainly *was* disturbed by the scalding liquid which poured on to his nose and the chair, thudding down on his tail. He leapt up, yowling, smashed his head against the bottom of the table and sent the whole lot crashing to the floor. Dazed, frightened and in pain, Herbert stood there barking. His body trembled, and a pool of water appeared on the lino beneath him.

'That is the last straw!' Mum yelled furiously. She raced to the bottom of the stairs. 'GRAN'MA!!' she screeched, and proceeded to storm up the stairs with the four of us chasing after her.

Without even pausing to knock, Mum burst in through the attic door. Seeing Gran'ma hunched up on the floor with her back to us and the radio spewing smoke, Mum put two and two together and came up with five.

'If you wanted a plug put on, you only

needed to ask,' she shouted. 'As if I haven't got enough to contend with, without you trying to blow us all up. Who do you think you are? Guy Fawkes?'

Gran'ma twisted round. Her pink face was smudged with soot and her long white hair — having escaped its bun — was hanging down in wispy strands. She blinked at us like a startled owl.

'I am quite capable of changing a plug,' she said, with as much dignity as she could muster.

'Capable?' Mum shouted. 'Don't make me laugh.'

We knew what she meant. Gran'ma had found it difficult to come to terms with the various electrical devices around the house. She'd destroyed the microwave attempting to make Yorkshire pudding in a metal baking tray. She'd mistaken the

Flymo for the Hoover and carved huge semi-circular gashes in the sitting-room carpet. And, completely misunderstanding how a video recorder works, she'd jammed it up permanently with a copy of *Jane Eyre*, her favourite book. Now the radio was also broken.

Gran'ma picked herself up, brushed herself down and stared at Mum with her piercing blue eyes.

'Please don't talk to me like that in front of the children,' she said. 'It isn't nice.'

Mum's jaw dropped open in amazement, which turned to anger, which turned to exasperation. She went to say something, thought better of it, turned on her heels and marched back down the stairs. 'Herbert!' she bellowed from the first landing. 'Heel! I do not want another accident on the carpet.'

Herbert remained where he was.

'Go on,' Richard said, nudging him with his foot and pointing to the door.

Reluctantly, Herbert did as he was told. Head down and tail between his legs, he shambled off.

'Wouldn't fancy being in *his* paws,' Gran'ma muttered.

We looked at Gran'ma Gillespie sadly. Herbert, at worst, would be banished to the garden; Gran'ma, on the other hand, was under threat of being sent to a retirement home. With yet another accident to add to the list, her removal to Bayview Towers was looking more likely than ever.

CHAPTER TWO

Radio Abracadabra

'What *did* happen to the radio?' Richard asked.

Gran'ma sighed. 'It's the reception here,' she complained irritably. 'I could hardly hear a thing. So I cast a spell,' she added, her eyes twinkling.

Richard, Harriet and I looked at one another uneasily. She was off on her *magic* thing again. Ever since my birthday the previous month, she had hardly talked about anything else.

Dad had brought me back a fantastic Magic Set from one of his last trips. It must have cost a packet, and I half-think he was trying to make up for it being two days late.

There were the props and step-by-step instructions for *ten thousand* magic tricks – not that I got much of a look in.

'It's a sign!' Gran'ma had said, and promptly commandeered the entire box. I'd only had the chance to try out one trick; and *that* hadn't worked. At least, not for Richard, Harriet or me.

It was the trick where you make a silk handkerchief change colour. You had to push it into your fist from one side, say the magic words – *Abracadabra, different hue; Take the red and turn it blue* – and then pull it out the other side, a different colour. Well, for us kids, nothing happened. The handkerchief remained stubbornly red.

Gran'ma's attempt was more successful. True, she didn't manage to turn it blue, but yellow, we thought, was just as clever. It was only later that we realized this first

performance showed *two* important facts. Gran'ma *was* able to do magic, but — and it was a big *but* — her tricks would not always go 100 per cent the way they should.

'So what was the spell?' I asked.

'For the radio?' she said.

I nodded.

'A simple one,' she said, and repeated it in a low whisper — so that the radio couldn't eavesdrop!

> 'Abracadabra
> Can't quite hear.
> Make this wireless
> Loud and clear.'

I looked at the radio. It occurred to me that it *had* been loud and clear — if only for a moment. The light on the tuner was still on, so it couldn't be completely broken. And I noticed something else: the dot on the volume button was pointing towards zero. I reached forward and turned it up. The room was filled with the sound of crackling static.

'*There* it is!' Gran'ma exclaimed. 'You clever boy!' she said and kissed me on the forehead. The next instant, she was off, jig-ging round the room and breathlessly sing-ing: *diddle dum dum, diddle dum dum, diddle diddle diddle diddle diddle dum dum.* 'Oh, "The Cauldron Gavotte",' she panted. 'They don't write songs like that any more.'

Richard and I stared in horror as Gran'ma continued to dance to the static. Harriet began to cry.

'My dears,' she said, seeing our distress and crouching down beside us. 'What *is* it?'

Harriet merely howled all the louder. Gran'ma gave her a hug and looked up at me sheepishly. 'I just felt like dancing,' she said. 'It was the music.'

'*What* music?' Richard and I demanded.

Gran'ma looked at us, one after the other. 'You can't hear it?' she said thoughtfully.

We all shook our heads. Gran'ma sat herself down on the carpet; we sat down beside her.

'I should explain,' she said slowly. 'A long time ago I used to do a lot of magic. But your grandad, God rest his soul, didn't like it. We lived in a very superstitious little village, you see. He didn't want me to stand out.'

'Are you a witch, Gran'ma?' Harriet asked, eyes wide.

'Let's just say, I have a certain power,' she said. 'A power which would not go away, no matter how hard I tried to deny it. When I saw the Magic Set, I knew that the move to your house was all part of a greater plan.'

Richard and I looked at one another. Mum and Dad had told us Gran'ma was moving in because she could no longer cope on her own — that, after the fire, her neighbours had alerted the social services. But Gran'ma clearly saw things differently.

'I was *meant* to come and live with you

18

all,' she explained. 'To sort out the silly mess Peter – your father – has got himself into. He shouldn't be away so often.'

We all agreed. These days we talked to him more on the telephone than face to face.

TELEPHONE DIRECTORY

'But how can *you* change anything?' I asked.

Gran'ma smiled. 'With a bit of magic,' she said. 'The trouble is, I'm rather rusty. And *that's* why I was trying to listen to the radio,' she said, glancing at her watch. 'There used to be a *Today's Spells* slot at six. I just wondered if I was still up to it. Once upon a time it would have been a piece of cake,' she added sadly.

'But why can't *we* hear the music?' Richard asked, and I could tell from the tone in his voice that he didn't believe a word of Gran'ma's story. But *I* did.

My earliest memory was of staying at Gran'ma's. It was when Richard was born, and I was three years old. I remember I'd just helped her to put out the washing, when suddenly it started to pour with rain.

'Wouldn't you believe it?' Gran'ma had said. Then, as I looked on, giggling, the pegs flew off the line and back into their bag; the sheets, shirts, skirts and dungarees all flapped up into the air, where they folded themselves neatly and came to rest on Gran'ma's outstretched arms. What was more, not only were they all bone dry, but they would not need ironing.

Gran'ma had merely smiled. 'Don't tell Grandad,' she'd said.

Yes, I believed her. And when she explained that Radio Abracadabra was only for the ears of those with the *power*, I believed that too. But this didn't make me feel any better. Far from it. Gran'ma was clearly no longer in full control of that power, and I was frightened of what damage she might unwittingly cause. Meaning well simply wasn't enough.

CHAPTER THREE

The Rat in the Hat

'It is a shame you can't hear,' Gran'ma said, as she climbed to her feet. 'You'd love "The Witches' Waltz".'

'That's what's playing now, is it?' Richard taunted.

'Actually, it's just finished,' said Gran'ma calmly as she smoothed down her clothes. She glanced at her watch again. 'It should . . . Yes. Here it comes!'

'*Today's Spells*?' I asked.

Gran'ma nodded excitedly and motioned us to sit down on the bed.

'A bit of hush, please,' she said, as she opened the Magic Set – *my* Magic Set! – placed it on the table and removed a length of cord. 'I need silence to concentrate.'

Silence was one thing Gran'ma didn't need to ask for. We sat there, well, *spellbound*, as she set to work. I looked round at the others. Harriet was biting into her lower lip nervously. Richard was smirking — I knew he thought Gran'ma was completely bonkers.

Certainly, she looked odd. A small, angular old woman with her wispy tangle of white hair, standing in the middle of the room, ear cocked towards the radio, muttering bits and pieces of the instructions only she could hear. In her tweed skirt and fluffy cardigan, she looked as *unlike* a witch as you could ever imagine.

'. . . fold twice, thrice, frice . . .' she said, as she awkwardly doubled and redoubled the cord. '. . . then cut . . . Cut, cut,' she repeated,

her fingers snipping at the air. She looked round. 'Thomas, my scissors are on the mantelpiece. Could you . . .?'

I was up before she'd finished her request.

'Thank you,' she said. 'Now . . . cut . . .' and she sliced through each of the sixteen loops. Thirty-two stubby ends appeared. Then she rolled up all the cut lengths of cord in her hand and, pausing to check with the radio, she repeated the magic words.

'Abracadabra
Deed be done,
Bits and pieces
All are one.'

With that, she pulled the cord from her closed hand. It had returned to its original length. Even Richard was impressed. But Gran'ma was not finished yet. She pulled out a second cord. And a third. And a fourth . . .

And as she continued to lay the shiny, white pieces down on the table, we realized that they didn't look quite like cord at all.

'It's spaghetti!' Harriet exclaimed, and started chuckling. At three years old, she thought it was funny. Richard, on the other hand, at almost seven, was old enough to understand that something very odd was going on. He nudged me.

'Do you think she *is* a witch?' he whispered. 'A *real* one?'

'What do *you* think?' I said.

Richard shook his head. 'This is really weird,' he muttered.

Gran'ma was staring at the heap of pasta with obvious irritation. However, she took a deep breath, and wiping her hands together, she said, 'Spell number two.'

'The dove number. This should be easy

enough. Take silk scarf, and place on your . . .
my hand, yes. Say . . . magic words.

> *Abracadabra*
> *Whistle and sing,*
> *A flight of fancy*
> *A bird on the wing.'*

The scarf immediately began to flutter as something beneath it stirred. Success, I thought. But I was wrong. When Gran'ma pulled back the scarf, a ferocious hawk with glinting eyes and savage talons caught us *all* by surprise. Harriet screamed.

'Oh dear!' Gran'ma groaned as the hawk flapped its wings and soared twice around the room before coming to rest on the curtain rail. 'I must be more out of practice than I'd thought. Third time lucky – I hope!' she added as, once again, she turned her attention to the radio.

'Take top hat ...' she said. 'A top hat? Who has a top hat these days?' She stomped over to the door and snatched her beret from the hook. 'This'll have to do,' she said. 'Now ... where was I?

> *Abracadabra*
> *Soft and pale,*
> *Loppy ears and*
> *Floppy tail.'*

She thrust her hand into the beret and held up the animal which had appeared. We had all seen enough magic shows before to know that the creature in her hand *should* have been a fluffy, white bunny with twitching whiskers and pink eyes. Or perhaps the dove which had failed to materialize in her previous trick. Certainly it should not have been a rat.

But a rat is what Gran'ma was clutching.

'Ugh,' she shuddered, and dropped it on to the table.

We watched as the sleek, brown animal sniffed at the air and scuttled over to the spaghetti, where it began gobbling down the sticky strands in great, greedy mouthfuls.

'Make it go away!' Harriet screamed. 'I hate rats.'

'Me too,' Gran'ma confessed as she scratched her head and racked her brain for a Disappearing Rat Spell.

There was only one creature in the room that didn't hate rats, and that was the hawk. It glared down greedily at the plump body, and launched itself off from the curtain rail. The rat glanced up, squeaked with terror and leapt from the table.

Harriet, Richard and I jumped up on to the bed as the rat scurried this way and that, in search of a place to hide from its attacker.

The hawk squawked and dived at the petri-
fied animal, legs outstretched.

'Eeeegh,' squealed the rat, as razor-sharp
talons scraped across its back.

'Waaarch,' screeched the hawk furiously,
as it realized its lunch had got away.

Unfortunately for us, it chose to hide
under the bed. And with the rat squeaking
beneath us and the hawk flapping above, it
all became too much. Harriet began yelling
first, then Richard started up, and before I
knew it, I too was screaming at Gran'ma to
make them stop, or disappear – or both.

At that moment, the door burst open. It
was Mum again.

'What on earth do you think you're playing a . . . aaarrgh!' she screamed, as the rat
scuttled across her slipper. Seeing the light
from the landing, it had decided to make a
run for it. And as the hawk watched its

quarry escaping, it had folded its wings and zoomed after in hot pursuit.

The three of us jumped off the bed and belted downstairs after the fleeing rat. Time and again, we saw the hawk dive in vain. With each attack, the rat managed to dodge out of the way, and the angry bird would fly back upwards with its talons full of tufts of carpet.

As we skidded into the kitchen, an agonized scream halted us in our tracks. The hawk had finally struck lucky. Screeching triumphantly, it flapped its wings and soared out of the open window with the hapless rat wriggling helplessly in its vice-like grip.

They were gone. And to make sure they remained gone, I slammed the window shut.

The damage, however, had already been done. We could hear Mum upstairs.

'Any *normal* grandmother would have a budgie or a cat as a pet,' she was shouting. 'But not you. Oh, no! You have to have a rat and a vulture.'

'It was a sparrow-hawk,' we heard Gran'ma explaining.

But Mum was having none of it.

'I will *not* have my house infested with vermin,' she shrieked. 'I'm telling you now: this is your very last warning!'

CHAPTER FOUR

In the Doghouse

Herbert was in disgrace once again. The screeching hawk and screaming rat had alarmed him and, cowering under the table, he had done what he always did when alarmed. Mum had returned to the kitchen after her set-to with Gran'ma to find Herbert padding wet footprints all over the lino.

It was over breakfast the following morning that Mum announced her decision. Herbert was old and poorly, she explained. Putting him to sleep would be the kindest thing all round.

'Will he be better when he wakes up?' Harriet asked innocently.

'He *won't* wake up,' said Richard angrily.

'Ever,' I added, glancing over at Herbert himself. He seemed to know that we were talking about him, and put his head on one side as if to ask what was going on. I looked away. His sad, trusting gaze was too much to bear.

'Are you going to take him now?' I asked bitterly.

'On Monday,' came Mum's reply, as she stacked our empty cereal bowls and took them over to the sink.

Richard leant forward. 'Let's get Gran'ma to have a look at him,' he whispered. 'She'll be able to cure him with a spell.'

'I didn't think you believed she could do magic,' I whispered back.

'I've changed my mind,' he replied.

'I don't know what you're plotting,' Mum said sharply. 'But I'm afraid it won't work. My mind is made up.'

Since Herbert had been banned from the carpeted areas of the house – which was everywhere except for the kitchen – we had to wait till Mum went out shopping before sneaking him upstairs.

At first, Gran'ma seemed reluctant to help.

'You saw what happened yesterday,' she said. 'I'm a lot rustier than I'd hoped.'

Only when we explained that it really was a matter of life and death, did she begin to relent.

'Anyway,' I said. 'If you *can* make him better, Mum might let *you* stay as well.'

Although Gran'ma clearly didn't like her situation being compared with that of a dog, she could see I had a point. She patted Herbert's head and crouched down beside him.

'Now why don't you start by telling me what's wrong?' she said.

Herbert sat himself down, raised his head

and howled mournfully.

'Hmmm,' Gran'ma said, stroking her chin. 'I see.'

Harriet, Richard and I simply stared. A rat in a hat was one thing, but talking dogs? Unaware of our reaction, however, Gran'ma took down a huge black book from the shelf. Richard and I read the title on the spine.

'What does it say?' Harriet demanded to know.

'Encyclopaedia of Spells, Charms and Remedies,' we replied, as Gran'ma flicked through the yellowed pages.

'Ah-ha!' she said finally. 'This ought to do it.

> *Abracadabra*
> *No more pain,*
> *Make this dog*
> *As right as rain!'*

As she clapped her hands together, a deafening roll of thunder echoed round the room. The next moment, a thick cloud swirling around the ceiling burst, and we found ourselves in the middle of a torrential rainstorm.

'ARBADACARBA!' Gran'ma roared, and raised her hands. The rain stopped and Herbert reappeared. He looked around groggily.

'Well, at least I seem to have got the hang of the *end-of-spell* command,' she said. 'Let

me see,' she added. 'What about this one?

Abracadabra
Nose, tail, paw:
Not off-colour
Any more.'

Once again, the spell had a dramatic effect. Once again, it was the wrong effect. Certainly, Herbert was no longer *off-colour*. In fact, with his red, orange, yellow, green, blue, violet and indigo stripes, he couldn't have been more *on-colour*. Having been a rainstorm, Herbert had now become the rainbow.

'Drat!' Gran'ma muttered, and changed him back.

Poor Herbert hadn't a clue what was going on. He stood there, whimpering pitifully and looking poorlier than ever. I was beginning to wonder whether it wouldn't be kinder to take him to the vet after all.

'There's one more spell I could try,' said Gran'ma, with a grin. 'I have the feeling it could be third time lucky.

> *Abracadabra*
> *No more piddle;*
> *Make this dog*
> *As fit as a fiddle!'*

As we burst out laughing, Herbert disappeared for a second time. Lying in his place was a violin.

'That's more like it,' said Gran'ma. 'Now, let's see,' she said, reading from her book once more. '*Play violin.*'

She picked up the instrument and ran the bow over the strings. The noise was horrible: almost as bad as Herbert's night-time howling.

'As I suspected,' said Gran'ma. 'You see, a

pet is like a car. Sometimes it needs a bit of fine tuning.'

And with that, she plucked at the strings and turned the knobs at the end of the neck until the violin was once again perfectly in tune. 'That should do it,' she said, as she played a sprightly jig. *That's* "The Cauldron Gavotte",' she announced. 'Charming, isn't it?'

'Great,' said Richard. 'But where's Herbert?'

'Whoops!' said Gran'ma. 'Silly me.' She returned the violin and bow to the carpet, checked the spell in the book and repeated it.

'Abracadabra
Don't be slack,
Healthy Rover
Welcome back!'

Nothing happened. For an awful moment we thought that we'd never see Herbert again. A pet violin wouldn't be much good at fetching sticks. Then again, neither was Herbert.

It was Harriet who realized what had gone wrong. 'He's not called Rover,' she said simply.

Gran'ma reread the spell. 'There's an asterisk next to Rover,' she muttered. 'Let me . . . Ah, yes! *Insert relevant name*. I see,' she said, and proceeded to repeat the spell, this time with Healthy *Herbert*.

Herbert promptly appeared, and from the way he started leaping around, wagging his tail and licking at our faces, we knew at once that he had made a complete recovery.

'You're wonderful!' Harriet shrieked, and gave Gran'ma a huge hug.

'Yeah, that was brilliant,' I said.

Gran'ma beamed at us happily. 'And you just wait,' she said. 'This is only the start. There are going to be one or two more changes in the Gillespie family.'

Her words sent a chill down my spine. Curing Herbert had proved difficult enough; I didn't like to think what might happen if she tried casting spells on *us*.

Richard, on the other hand, seemed only too willing to be experimented on. Ever since the episode with the hawk, he'd been bursting to ask her something. Finally, he could keep it in no longer.

'Can you make people *fly*?' he said. 'I've always wanted to,' he added bashfully.

Gran'ma smiled. 'Among other things,' she replied mysteriously.

CHAPTER FIVE

A Most Peculiar Picnic

Despite the promising answer to Richard's question, Gran'ma did not perform any more magic that Saturday. At least, not while *we* were around. Harriet, Richard and I, together with Herbert, found ourselves being bustled out of the room.

'Practice makes perfect,' Gran'ma explained. 'I need to polish up my act a little before I make my next move.'

Half of me was disappointed – I, too, had always wanted to fly. The other half, however, was relieved. It was reassuring to discover that Gran'ma recognized her own limitations. What I didn't then realize was just how much practice she would actually need.

From that moment on, she kept herself locked up in her attic bedroom, refusing to emerge, even at mealtimes. At first, it was all a bit of a joke.

'It's just as well there's a toilet up there,' Richard said, and burst out laughing.

But as the days passed, we began to wonder if we'd ever see Gran'ma again. Even Mum was concerned. Three times a day, she would leave a tray, laden with food, outside

Gran'ma's door. Three times a day, she would bring it back downstairs – untouched.

Occasionally, one or other of us would knock on her door to check that she was all right. But the answer was always the same.

'I am *perfectly* well, thank you,' she would say. 'Just leave me in peace.'

Once, when *I* asked her, I could have sworn she was talking with her mouth full.

'Perhaps she's practising Food Spells,' said Richard, when I told him.

It was that Friday that we discovered how right Richard had been. Gran'ma breezed into the room for breakfast as though nothing had happened. Herbert stood up and wagged his tail excitedly. Mum's reaction was less enthusiastic.

'What *have* you been doing all this time?' she snapped.

Gran'ma merely smiled. 'All will be

revealed at the end of the month,' she said cryptically, and before anyone could say another word, she had changed the subject. 'Why don't we all go on a picnic?' she suggested. 'It's such a lovely day.'

'Oh, yes!' we all shouted. 'Can we, Mum? Can we?'

Mum looked at Gran'ma irritably. 'I've got so much on my plate,' she complained.

'*I'll* eat it,' Harriet offered.

Mum grinned.

'You haven't had much of a holiday, have you?' she said, turning to Richard and me.

We shook our heads. First Dad, and then the weather, had let us down. Today was the first day of the half-term break that we hadn't woken up to grey skies and pouring rain.

'All right,' she said finally. 'But I'll need half an hour to pack up some food.'

'No need,' said Gran'ma. 'I've already taken care of all that.'

It took the best part of an hour to get outside the town and into the country.

Everyone else seemed to have had the same idea. Yet, when Mum pulled up at the edge of Hareton Wood, the picnic area was deserted.

'Wonderful,' Gran'ma murmured. 'Come on, let's go for a ramble. Build up an appetite,' she added, with a grin.

Normally, we didn't like boring walks. But today we made an exception – it was just nice being with Gran'ma again. So, with Herbert frisking round us like a puppy, we left the Frisbee and football in the back of the car and set off through the trees and into the fields. And as we walked, Gran'ma talked.

'This is feverfew,' she said, picking some daisy-like flowers. 'Just the job for a migraine. And that's thuja,' she said. 'Good for verrucae.'

And so it went on. There wasn't a flower, shrub or tree that Gran'ma didn't know the

name of, or medicinal use for. Even Mum was impressed.

'It's like taking a stroll with a walking encyclopaedia,' she laughed.

And suddenly I remembered the title on Gran'ma's huge black book. Spells, Charms *and Remedies*. So that was what she had been doing all that time. Studying.

'Look,' said Richard. 'A newt.'

'They too have their uses,' said Gran'ma, and winked.

By the time we got back to the car, we were all famished.

'Right,' said Gran'ma, taking control. 'Beth, you go and sit at the picnic table. We'll get the food ready, won't we, kids?'

'But . . .' Mum began.

'Do as you're told!' Gran'ma said sharply. 'It's your day off. There's no need for her to know about the magic,' she whispered for our benefit, as she opened the boot.

We peered inside expectantly.

'Is that *it*?' Richard said, staring at the one small sandwich box it contained.

Gran'ma smiled to herself. 'A little bit of faith wouldn't come amiss, young man,' she chided.

> *'Abracadabra*
> *Off the shelf —*
> *A feast as sweet*
> *As life itself.'*

She opened the lid, put in her hand and pulled out a table-cloth, plates, napkins, glasses, salt and pepper pots, knives, forks and spoons.

'Go and lay the table, there's a dear,' she said to me.

Before I'd finished, Harriet and Richard were already bringing over plateloads of

food. There were tomatoes, boiled eggs, but-
tered rolls, sticks of celery and a cucumber;
crisps, crackers and a tin of biscuits, a huge
wedge of Cheddar and a joint of ham. And
when I got back to the car, Gran'ma was
holding out a large bowl.

'Raspberry and banana trifle,' she announced.

I stared at it in disbelief. The bowl was at least twice as big as the box it had come from. Gran'ma smiled.

'A witch in time saves nine,' she said,

plunging her arm deep into the box and removing an impossibly large bottle – and an even more impossibly large box of ice.

'Nothing worse than warm lemonade,' she observed, as she followed me to the table.

Ignoring our questioning stares, Gran'ma clinked ice-cubes into each of the glasses, poured in the frothy lemonade and handed them round.

'Cheers,' she said.

'Who'd have thought we'd be having a picnic in the middle of October?' Mum commented as we raised our glasses.

October. That's it! I realized. Gran'ma had said that all would be revealed at the end of the month. It had suddenly occurred to me just what that meant, but before I had a chance to say anything, I was interrupted.

'Ugh!' Mum exclaimed, and spat out her

mouthful of lemonade. 'That is disgusting!'

We all looked at her curiously. *Our* lemonade was the best we'd ever tasted. Fresh lemons, honey, a dash of peaches and a hint of lime: it was delicious.

'It's so sour!' she winced.

'It all came out of the same bottle,' said Gran'ma.

'I know,' said Mum, looking puzzled. 'Thomas, what do you think of it?'

'It's lovely,' I replied, equally puzzled.

Everything Gran'ma had produced from the sandwich box tasted fantastic: nothing tasted as it should. The sausage rolls didn't contain sausage at all, but a thick roll of chocolate. The hard-boiled eggs, once shelled, were ice-cream with a marzipan centre. And the rolls — with cheese in them — tasted of lemon meringue pie. It was the sweetest, gooiest, deliciousest picnic we had ever had. Yet, as we tucked in,

Mum merely looked on, unconvinced.

'Not hungry?' Gran'ma asked.

'I ...' She nibbled her tomato half-heartedly, and immediately screwed up her nose. 'Vinegar!' she said. 'Gran'ma, this is foul!'

'Vinegar,' Gran'ma repeated thoughtfully. 'What about the rest of you?'

We all bit into *our* tomatoes. They were wonderful: sweet, juicy and nothing at all like tomato.

'Strawberries and cream,' Harriet exclaimed.

'Strawberries and cream!' Mum exploded. 'That's it. I've had enough.'

'Where are you going?' I asked.

'To get a mint from the glove compartment,' she said. 'I need something to get rid of the vile taste in my mouth.'

'What was all that about?' Richard said, when she was out of earshot.

'Yeah,' I said. 'Why didn't Mum like the

food?'

Gran'ma shook her head sadly. '*You* heard the spell,' she said finally. 'I can only conclude that life, for your mum, is simply not quite sweet enough. Not like Herbert!' she added. Herbert was gnawing at his bone as if it was a juicy steak. Gran'ma looked thoughtful. 'I didn't realize things were quite so serious,' she said.

'Can't you do something?' Harriet asked.

Gran'ma smiled weakly. 'One way or another,' she said. 'But not just now. You'll have to wait till the end of the . . .'

'Hallowe'en!' I said, remembering what I'd thought of earlier.

'Yes,' Gran'ma replied, her eyes twinkling. 'Hallowe'en.'

CHAPTER SIX

Hallowe'en Night

Gran'ma was more upset by the way the picnic turned out than we realized at first. She had wanted to make amends; she had wanted to give us a treat. *All* of us. Instead, her magic had gone wrong again, and Mum was left feeling worse than ever.

'Back to the drawing-board,' Gran'ma muttered when we got home, and promptly disappeared back up to her room.

The days passed. Richard and I went back to school; Dad returned, and went away again – to New York this time; and though Gran'ma did emerge now and then, for meals and the occasional bedtime story, she refused to do any more magic.

'I thought you were going to make us fly?' Richard complained one evening.

'Trying to run – or fly – before you can walk is not to be advised,' Gran'ma said firmly.

'But . . .' we all protested.

'All things come to those who wait,' Gran'ma interrupted, and smiled.

And with that, the conversation was at a close. We had no option but to wait.

By the time the end of the month did finally arrive we were so busy with our Penny for the Guy that we'd forgotten all about Hallowe'en. It was only when we were getting ready for bed that I suddenly remembered what day it was – and by then, it was too late. Gran'ma had gone out shortly after breakfast and had still not returned by suppertime.

I don't remember falling asleep, but I

suppose I must have, because I *do* remember being woken up.

'Gran'ma,' I mumbled, opening my eyes.

'Ssshhh!' she whispered. 'Don't make a sound. Get the others up and meet me in the garden. I sense magic in the air!'

Before I had a chance to ask what was going on, Gran'ma was gone.

By the light of the full moon, I dressed, woke the others and together we tiptoed downstairs and out of the back door. Bathed in the silvery moonlight, the garden certainly *looked* magical.

'She's down there,' I said, pointing to a shadowy figure near the bottom fence. Bleary-eyed and shivery, we crossed the sparkling lawn towards her.

'Ah, there you are,' Gran'ma said, looking up.

Harriet gasped. Richard sniggered.

Perched upon Gran'ma's head – and looking
quite ridiculous with her tartan overcoat –
was a black, pointed hat. She began to utter
curious words:

'When full moon falls on All Hallows' Eve

Be ye prepared, the power to receive;

What can happen, shall happen, if ye believe

When full moon falls on All Hallows' Eve.

'It helps to funnel the energy,' she added, and grinned. 'I need all the help I can get.'

'I thought the power was inside you,' I said.

'Inside, outside; it is the same,' said Gran'ma. 'On Hallowe'en night there is more magic about than at any other time of the year. 'Accordingly, I too am at my most powerful.'

Shivers ran up and down my back as I remembered all the spells that had already gone that little bit wrong. I had the horrible feeling that, with *more* power at her disposal, Gran'ma would now be able to make them go *completely* wrong. But Gran'ma herself seemed unconcerned.

'Tonight, my dears, your wishes will all come tru . . .' She stopped, and squinted past us, up at the house.

We turned, and immediately saw what

had caught her attention. Up in Mum and Dad's bedroom, the tell-tale darting yellow of torchlight was bouncing about behind the curtains.

'A burgular!' Harriet said.

'*Burg-u-lar!*' Richard sneered.

'Be quiet, you two,' Gran'ma snapped. 'Your mum's on her own up there. This is serious.'

Harriet and Richard fell silent, and we all watched as Gran'ma strode to the middle of the lawn. There, she stopped, adjusted her hat, raised her hands and whispered something under her breath.

Although we couldn't hear the spell, we saw the result all right. As Gran'ma clapped her hands together, the bedroom window burst open and a tall, thin man flew out and proceeded to spin and somersault through the air, just like a balloon that slips out of your fingers before you've knotted it.

'Whoops,' Gran'ma muttered as she tried to steady her outstretched fingers. At that moment, the pointed hat threatened to topple

off her head. Instinctively, her hands shot up to steady it, and as they did so, the flying man soared up into the sky and out of view.

'Aaaa-iiii!' he squealed, his anguished cry growing softer by the second.

'Do you think she's put him into orbit?' I heard Richard whisper worriedly.

I shook my head. 'No idea,' I said.

One thing was clear. Gran'ma was having problems getting the burglar back down. She kept pointing to different places in the sky, and beckoning. It was only on her ninth or tenth attempt that she finally struck lucky. We heard the faint but unmistakable sound of terrified screaming way above our heads. And, looking up, we saw the tiny dot of a man as he hurtled down towards the ground.

My heart raced furiously as I realized how right I'd been to fear Gran'ma's Hallowe'en powers.

That could be me, I thought, horrified.

Gran'ma, for her part, continued to hold her arms up to the sky and, as the man drew nearer, she suddenly twisted her hands round so that her palms were up. The effect was instantaneous. The man's fall was abruptly broken. He hovered in mid-air for a moment before completing his descent, like an autumn leaf floating gently down to earth. Or rather, *almost* down to earth. At Gran'ma's command, he had come to rest a couple of centimetres above the grass.

We watched the man wipe his brow and rub his eyes. He looked up into the sky and shook his head.

'No,' we heard him say. 'Must have been something I ate. That Chicken Tikka was past its sell-by date.'

Then, having checked his bulging pockets, he set off. At least, he tried to set off. But

although his legs moved more and more furiously, the burglar remained in precisely the same spot. Confused, he stopped and looked down. It was then he noticed the two-centimetre gap beneath him.

'Aaargh!' he screamed. 'This is a night-mare.'

'Of your own making,' Gran'ma proclaimed, as she marched towards the immobilized burglar.

'Where did you lot come from?' the man gasped, as he found himself confronted by three kids and an old woman in a silly hat.

'Thomas,' Gran'ma said, ignoring him. 'Would you please go and call the police.'

'No, not the police,' he shouted. 'Here,' he said, pulling Mum's necklaces, bracelets, brooches and rings from his pocket. He tossed them to the ground.

But Gran'ma was unimpressed. 'Go on, Thomas,' she said. 'And ask them to come round the back way. I don't want your mum woken.'

As I sped off towards the kitchen, I could

hear the burglar still trying to change her mind. *Please* take them,' he begged her. 'I didn't mean to. I've been under a lot of stress recently. I'm not well. Honest!'

It was only the approaching siren and flashing blue light that finally put an end to his pleading. As the police constables came running across the lawn towards us, Gran'ma

clicked her fingers and the man collapsed on to the lawn.

'We caught him in the act of burglary,' Gran'ma explained. 'Red-handed. Here is the evidence,' she said, retrieving the jewels from the grass.

The policeman looked at the burglar.

'Have you anything to say?' he asked.

'I need a doctor,' he replied weakly.

At that moment Mum, who had been woken by the raised voices and wailing siren, appeared at the kitchen door in her dressing-gown. She stood on the step and looked round the semi-circle of people gathered in front of her: at the policeman, at the tall, thin man, at the policewoman, at Gran'ma — still clutching the jewellery — at Harriet, at Richard, at me.

'What on earth is going on?' she demanded to know. 'And why are you three dressed?'

Suddenly everyone was talking at the same time. No one could make themselves heard. Mum clamped her hands over her ears.

'Enough!' she shouted. 'We'll discuss this inside,' she said to the police constables. 'And Thomas, Richard, Harriet, I want *you* to go back to bed.'

'Oh, Mu-um,' we all moaned.

'NOW!!' she roared.

Mum was clearly in no mood for arguments. We filed past her, obedient but dejected. The night we had been so looking forward to had proved a complete disaster — and, judging by the expression on Mum's face, the following morning promised to be even worse.

CHAPTER SEVEN

The Family Photograph

'Stupid thing,' I said to Herbert, when I came downstairs the next morning. 'Some guard dog you turned out to be.'

Herbert looked up at me questioningly, head on one side. He wagged his tail, and I hadn't the heart to remain angry. It wasn't his fault he had slept through the commotion of the previous night. But if only he *had* woken up to the intruder, then maybe we would have got to fly after all. I realized sadly that with Hallowe'en night now over, we would probably have to wait a whole year before getting another opportunity.

Mum, on the other hand, was happier than I expected. Relieved that the burglar hadn't managed to steal anything, she seemed to forget all about the fact that she'd found us dressed. I didn't even need to explain how we heard a noise downstairs, put our clothes on because it was cold, and came down to investigate — which was just as well, really. I don't like telling lies. They always seem to get you into more trouble than they get you out of.

As for Gran'ma, she was the heroine of the hour. If Mum had been sceptical that she'd been responsible for Herbert's miraculous recovery, she was certainly in no doubt that Gran'ma had thwarted the burglary. She couldn't do enough for her: breakfast in bed, a bunch of flowers in her room and spaghetti Bolognese — her favourite — for Sunday dinner. What was more, there was no more talk of Bayview Towers.

It was late afternoon and Richard, Harriet

and I were in the garden playing football
when we heard a familiar *honk-di-HONK*. Dad
was home! Interrupting our game, we raced
round to the front of the house to greet him.
Mum and Gran'ma were already there.

'I wasn't expecting you back till Wednes-
day,' Mum was saying. 'At the earliest!'

Dad grinned. 'Promotion,' he said.

'Promotion!' we all exclaimed.

'What's promoshin?' asked Harriet quietly.

Dad crouched beside her. 'It means that Daddy won't be going on any more trips abroad,' he said. 'From now on, I'll be home every evening and every weekend. I heard last night,' he added, looking up at the rest of us. 'Totally out of the blue.'

I glanced at Gran'ma. She was saying nothing, but from the smug expression on her face, I was convinced that she'd had something to do with the news. After all, hadn't she said that Dad shouldn't be away so often; hadn't she claimed that she had come to stay in order to sort out his 'silly mess', as she called it.

It was only when we were back inside that Gran'ma finally spoke.

'I think Peter's wonderful news calls for a celebration,' she said. 'It's a bit early for champagne, but I think some elderflower fizz should do the trick.' And so saying, she produced a large bottle and six glasses, apparently out of nowhere.

Mum stared down at her glass of bubbly suspiciously. She remembered all too well the lemonade she'd had on the picnic.

'To the Gillespies,' Gran'ma said, raising her glass. 'Each and every one!'

'Each and every one!' we all echoed, and sipped at our drinks.

We thought it was fantastic — like

sparkling nectar. But what about Mum? We looked at her, half expecting to see her spitting it out. But no. A broad grin spread over her face.

'This is absolutely delicious,' she said.

Gran'ma smiled. 'I have the feeling that, from now on, life, for us all, is going to be that little bit sweeter.'

'I'll drink to that,' said Dad, as he drained his glass and placed it on the coffee-table. 'Now, if no one has any objections, I think I'll just have a shower.'

'I'll help you unpack,' Mum added.

'Oh, Da-ad,' we all moaned. 'Can't we just . . .'

'Come on, you lot,' Gran'ma interrupted. 'Let your parents have a couple of minutes on their own.'

'I promise we'll do anything you want this evening,' said Dad. 'Once I've got out of these clothes,' he said, sniffing at his armpit and wincing theatrically. 'Pooh!'

'Will you play Avenger with me on the computer?' I said.

'Could we put the train-set up?' Richard asked.

'Can you help me with my Alperbet Puzzle?' said Harriet.

Dad grinned. 'Anything you want,' he repeated.

As Mum and Dad left the sitting-room by one door, Gran'ma ushered us out through the other.

'Where are we going?' Richard asked.

'Unfinished business,' Gran'ma replied mysteriously.

It was already dark as we trooped out into the garden. The sun had set, but the moon was not yet up, and it had become so cold that you could see your breath. We stood, shivering on the wet grass, wondering what was going on.

'Right,' Gran'ma instructed. 'Stand in a line over there. Now, don't fidget.'

'But what . . .?' Richard began.

'Or *talk*!' Gran'ma snapped.

She raised her hands until her fingers were pointing towards us. I remembered the last time I'd seen her doing that, and my heart started racing. Even with all the excitement of Dad coming back, Gran'ma hadn't forgotten about us.

> '*Abracadabra*
> *Up to the sky,*
> *Make Thomas and Richard*
> *And Harriet fly!*'

The spell sounded so simple. Too simple! And yet, even as I was busy doubting that it could ever work, something was beginning

to happen. A curious sensation filled my body; it started at my toes, shivered up my legs, set my stomach spinning and my fingers tingling. I felt dizzy. I felt light. I felt as if a million zillion tiny bubbles of lemonade — or elderflower fizz — were effervescing inside me.

Suddenly I realized I was floating. Like the burglar, I hovered above the ground. Unlike the burglar — who Gran'ma had first sent

hurtling into space and then fixed to the spot – I discovered that *I* was in control. By kicking my legs and flapping my arms, I could rise up as high as I chose.

I'd dreamt of being able to fly so often that I knew exactly what to do; and Richard and Harriet got the hang of it just as quickly. Before long, the three of us were soaring and swooping, wheeling and diving like birds.

'Wheee!' we squealed.

'Bravo!' Gran'ma shouted.

We flew in formation; we flew from tree to tree; we did cartwheels and somersaults in the air. Flying was the most wonderful feeling ever, and the three of us would have happily remained up in the air throughout the night. Sadly, as good things are apt to do, the flight came to an end all too soon.

'Come on down now,' Gran'ma said. 'Your mum and dad will be wondering where you are.'

And when we made no move to come in to land, she raised her hand towards us and clicked her fingers. Inside me, it felt as if the million zillion bubbles were bursting, one by one by one. It became harder and harder to remain airborne; gradually the three of us sank back to earth.

'Oh, just one more go,' we all clamoured.

Gran'ma smiled. 'There'll be other times,' she said.

Mum and Dad were already in the sitting-room when we got back. Mum was on the settee, with Herbert lying at her feet; Dad was lining up the camera on the table opposite.

'*There* you are,' he said, looking up. 'Just in time. Sit down all of you. In a bit, Gran'ma.

Lovely.'

He pressed the automatic button, raced over towards us and squeezed in between Mum and me.

'Smile!' he said.

The camera clicked and whirred, and a shiny, blank piece of paper emerged from the bottom. We all jumped up, and stood round as the photograph gradually developed.

And there we were: the Gillespie family, which – thanks to Gran'ma – was all together for once.

Looking at the happily grinning faces, it was hard to imagine that anything in our lives could ever go wrong again. But of course it did. Only four short days after the photograph was taken, Gran'ma cast a spell that went so horribly wrong that we were all plunged into yet another disaster.

But that, as they say, is another story.